The Bus Is

Michael Rosen

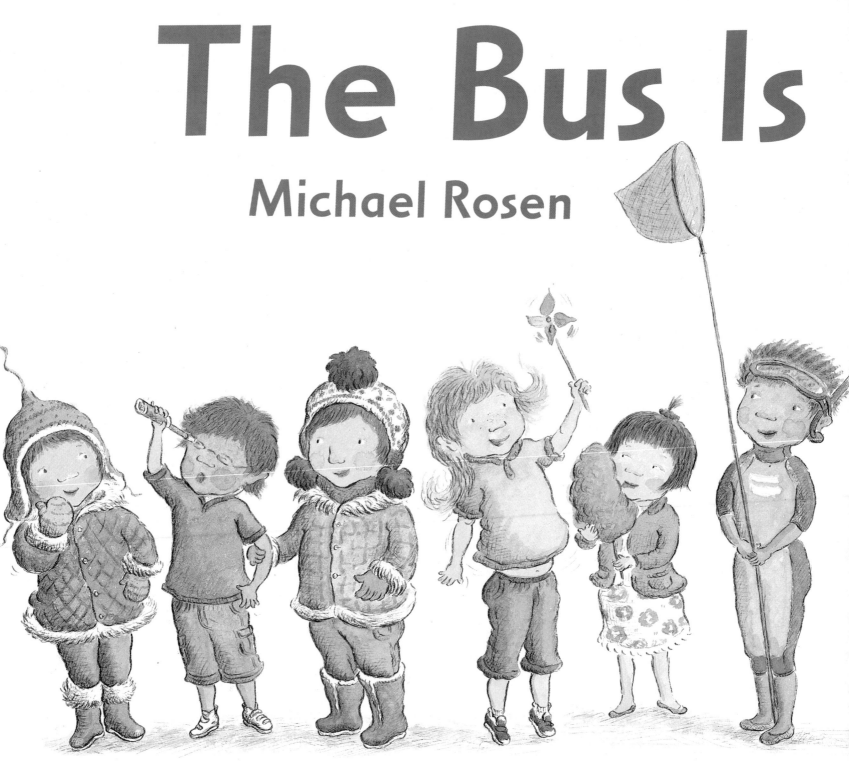

For Emma, Elsie and Emile... M.R. ✴ ∿ ✴ *For Frazer McGown love Aunty Gilly*

First published 2015 by Walker Books Ltd 87 Vauxhall Walk, London SE11 5HJ ◆ Text © 2015 Michael Rosen ◆ Illustrations © 2015 Gillian Tyler ◆ The right of Michael Rosen and Gillian Tyler to be identified as author and illustrator respectively of this work has been asserted by them in accordance with the Copyright, Designs and Patents Act 1988 ◆ This book has been typeset in AT Arta ◆ Printed in China ◆ All rights reserved. No part of this book may be reproduced, transmitted or stored in an information retrieval system in any form or by any means, graphic, electronic or mechanical, including photocopying, taping and recording, without prior written permission from the publisher.

British Library Cataloguing in Publication Data: a catalogue record for this book is available from the British Library ◆ ISBN 978-1-4063-3714-3 ◆ www.walker.co.uk ◆ 10 9 8 7 6 5 4 3 2 1

For Us!

Gillian Tyler

WALKER BOOKS

AND SUBSIDIARIES

LONDON • BOSTON • SYDNEY • AUCKLAND

I really like

to ride my bike

I like going far

in our car

YR2APY

When it

starts to rain

I like

the train.

But best is the bus.
The bus is for us.

I do of course
like riding a horse

I like to float

in a little boat

I like trips
in big ships.

But best is the bus.

**The bus
is for us.**

Sometimes I wish
I could ride on a fish

If I was allowed

I'd sit on a cloud

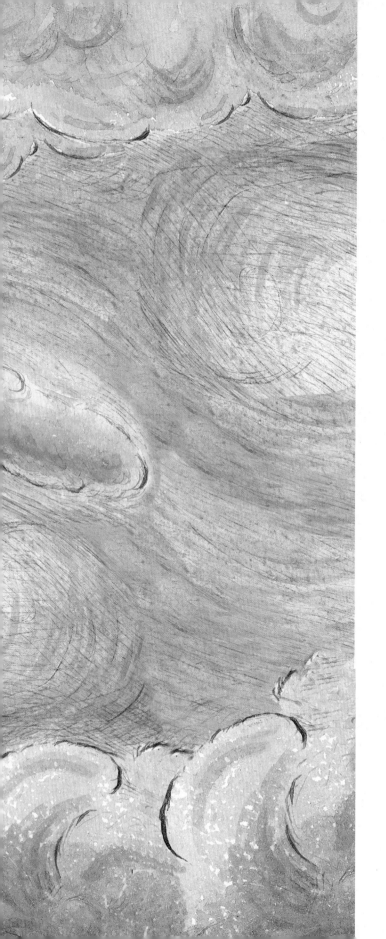

I'd be all right
up high on a kite.

But best is the bus.
The bus is for us.

I'd love to play

in an open sleigh

Fly to the moon
in a hot-air balloon

Or for a dare
ride on a bear.

But even so

the bus is best.

Best is the bus.

That's because

**the bus
is for US!**